Where Will You Swim Tonight?

Milly Jane Limmer

Illustrated by Helena Clare Pittman

ALBERT WHITMAN & COMPANY • Morton Grove, Illinois

To Richard, with thanks for the sea horse. M.J.L.
For Kay, dear friend, with much love. H.C.P.

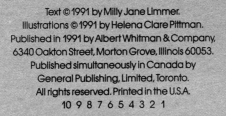

Text © 1991 by Milly Jane Limmer.
Illustrations © 1991 by Helena Clare Pittman.
Published in 1991 by Albert Whitman & Company,
6340 Oakton Street, Morton Grove, Illinois 60053.
Published simultaneously in Canada by
General Publishing, Limited, Toronto.
All rights reserved. Printed in the U.S.A.
10 9 8 7 6 5 4 3 2 1

Library of Congress Cataloging-in-Publication Data
Limmer, Milly Jane.
Where will you swim tonight?/Milly Jane Limmer;
illustrated by Helena Clare Pittman.
p. cm.
Summary: A bath time counting book in which a
girl grows a tail and swims along with one knobby
sea horse, two smooth dolphins, and other sea
creatures up to the number ten.
ISBN 0-8075-8949-7
[1. Baths—Fiction. 2. Marine animals—Fiction.
3. Counting. 4. Stories in rhyme.]
I. Pittman, Helena Clare, ill. II. Title.
PZ8.3.L6145Wh 1991   90-38938
[E]—dc20   CIP   AC

Typography and Cover Design:
Karen Johnson Campbell.

The illustrations are watercolor and pencil
on Strathmore Bristol Board Series 500.

The text typeface is Avant Garde Book.

If you were a fish, where
would you go?

Where would you swim?
Where would you play?

Where could you shimmy
with silvery fins
to merrily burble
and bubble all day?

With one knobby sea horse,
wandering into a hidden cave?

With two smooth dolphins,
   gliding through a hushing wave?

With three scratchy crabs,
scooting past a mermaid's home?

With four soft sea otters,

floating on the sparkling foam?

With five hard turtles,
    paddling over shadowy reeds?

With six prickly blowfish,

puffing between slow-swaying weeds?

With seven slippery eels,

slithering out of a sunken ship's hold?

With an eight-legged octopus,
   wrapped around a chest of gold?

With nine lumpy oysters,
   slumbering where their pale pearls glow?

With ten floppy penguins,
parading across an icy floe?

Now that you've been
beneath the waves

where dolphins sail
past secret caves
and turtles glide
through shimmering light...

can you tell me where you
will swim tonight?